My First Kisment Christmas

Cowboys of Sunnydale, Volume 5

Allie Bock

Published by Allie Bock, 2024.

Table of Contents

Prologue 1
Chapter One 4
Chapter Two 10
Chapter Three 20
Chapter Four 26
Chapter Five 33
Chapter Six 41
Chapter Seven 47
Chapter Eight 54
Chapter Nine 65
Chapter Ten 73
Epilogue 78

Copyright Page

Copyright © 2023 by Allie Bock
All rights reserved. No part of this publication may be reproduced, stored, or transmitted in any form or by any means, electronic, mechanical, photocopying, recording, scanning, or otherwise without written permission from the publisher. It is illegal to copy this book, post it to a website, or distribute it by any other means without permission.

This novel is entirely a work of fiction. The names, characters, and incidents portrayed in it are the work of the author's imagination. Any resemblance to actual persons, living or dead, events or localities is entirely coincidental.
Cover Design by Tugboat Design
First edition

Dedication

To all who found love the second time around

Books by Allie Bock

Cowboys of Sunnydale Series:
My Cowboy Crush
Falling for My Cowboy
Second Chance with My Bull Rider
My Unexpected Hero
My Cowboy of Convenience
My First Kisment Christmas
Find out more about Allie's books at:
Alliebock.com[1]
Alliebock.substack.com[2]

---

1. https://alliebock.com/
2. https://alliebock.substack.com/

Prologue

Judy

Present Day Christmas Eve

The living room of our ranch house was filled to the brim with my family. My daughter, Katie, handed Erin a box of Christmas ornaments.

"This is so cute!" Erin pulled out a hand print wreath that the children had made for me when they were in elementary school. She held it up in the direction of Kaleb, my firstborn, and her fiancee.

He nodded. A small smile tugged at the corner of his lips. His neck reddened under her gaze. "It was Kurt's idea."

All the women in the room turned to Kurt, my second oldest son. He lounged in the Lazy Boy chair. He shrugged and pulled his fiancee, Lindsay, closer into his lap. "Ma was so happy with us when she opened the box."

"We did something similar for my mom." Erin hung the ornament on the tree. "We painted pine cones with glue and rolled them in glitter to give to her...She wasn't thrilled." She dug in the box for another ornament. "She vacuumed glitter out of the carpet for months."

"I know the feeling," I said.

"It's only because we weren't into glitter, Ma." Kade, my youngest son, handed me a cup of hot chocolate.

"I'm thankful for that." I smiled at him. He winked back before distributing cups of hot chocolate to the rest of the family.

"Erin, what's your family doing today?" Tim, my husband, stood behind my chair. He dropped a hand onto my shoulder, squeezing it gently.

She hung an angel ornament on one of the top branches of the Christmas tee. "Mom said that it's supposed to snow buckets overnight."

"Snow." Kaleb shuddered.

"It isn't that bad." Erin grinned at him. "It was just a dusting at Thanksgiving. Anyway, Mom is baking pies and Dad is getting the tractor ready."

"Ready for what?" Katie draped tinsel over the branches.

"The snow. He digs all the neighbors out and delivers Mom's pies on Christmas Day. They do it every year." She stepped back from the tree.

Katie hung the last bit of tinsel. She put her hands on her hips and tilted her head. "We just need the star on top." She pulled it out from the box.

"That's my job." Tim took the star and placed at the top of the tree.

"Perfect." I clapped my hands together. It was a perfect. Tim and I were home from our mission trip. Our children were all there with their significant others. My house and heart couldn't be more filled.

"Ma, Erin hasn't heard your Christmas story yet." Katie folded herself into a sitting position, leaning back against her husband, Levi.

"It's been years since I've heard it, too," Delilah said as Kade came to stand behind her.

Tim smiled at me. My insides warmed at his look. Over thirty years together and he could still make me feel like the first time I met him.

"As long as your dad will help," I said.

"Of course, darling." He sat next to me and draped his arm over my shoulders. "Do you want me to start or you?"

"I always like how you start the story." I turned my face towards his.

He kissed my lips gently. "Alright then." His eyes pulled me in until it was just us all those years ago.

Chapter One

Tim

December 22nd Over thirty years ago

Bang! Pop! Hiss!

The noises came from the engine of my truck. It shuddered and white smoke billowed from under the hood.

"For Pete's sake," I muttered. "I don't need this right now."

I slapped the blinker on and gently pulled the truck and horse trailer to the side of the highway. In the trailer, the colts stomped and neighed causing it to rock from side to side.

This was just what I needed. My father bought these young horses and wanted them picked up today. Unfortunately, the pump for one of our wells went out and he was needed at home. I was designated to go in his place.

I turned the key, shutting the ignition off. Climbing out of the cab, I walked to the hood of the truck. Once it was opened, more of the white smoke poured out. Something dripped on to the ground.

"Just perfect." I ran my hand through my hair. I wasn't a mechanic and not technically inclined at all.

I stomped back to the trailer and looked inside. The four horses danced in their slots but appeared fine. A bale of hay sat in the bed of the truck along with other odds and ends from the farm. I cut the strings on the bale and gave each horse some more hay. The stomping settled down as they dug into the sweet smelling hay.

"Now what to do?" I scanned the horizon for any sign of people.

It was the stretch of highway where there was nothing but cacti, jackrabbits, and rocks. No people, no houses, no gas stations. Nothing. The nearest one I remember seeing was about forty miles back. It would take me forever to walk there and I couldn't leave the colts. None of them were broke to ride and Father paid a pretty penny for them.

I climbed into the bed of the truck, searching for anything that might help. The toolbox held fencing supplies, a coil of rope, and a warm six pack of beer. I chuckled at that. One of the ranch hands must have driven this truck last. None of it was going to help me. I sat down on the tailgate and decided to wait. Someone was bound to come along.

Forty minutes later, headlights shone in the distance. Then, a purr of an engine reached me. A little red sports car zoomed into view. I jumped down from the tailgate and walked to the back of the trailer. Raising my arms above my head, I prayed they would see me and stop.

The car slowed down and pulled over in front of my truck. The driver's door swung open.

"Thanks for stopping. I thought no one would..." The words caught in my throat at the woman exiting the car. Her red hair gleamed in the sun as it floated around her shoulders.

"You're welcome." She smiled at me, and my heart leapt into my throat. The smile faded as she took me in. She gasped. "No way. Tim?"

I nodded, feeling dazed at the vision before me.

"Who would have thought?" Her smile returned, beaming out at me, filling me with warmth.

"Judy White?" I stepped toward her. "What are you doing in Texas?" My hands reached for hers.

She grasped mine. A bolt of electricity shot through me, jump starting my heart. I slid my hands up her arms to rest at her shoulders.

"It's been so long." My voice came out in a whisper.

"Yep, almost ten years." She nodded.

I wanted to hug and kiss her, but the time span from when we were high school sweethearts to now prevented that.

"You're a sight for sore eyes." I stared into her eyes that transported me back to when I was eighteen years old.

She snorted. "Sure. Did you even look at me?"

My gaze tore from her eyes to traverse her face and then traveled down her body. Her hands went to cradle her burgeoning belly.

"You're pregnant?"

"It looks like it, doesn't it?" The corner of her lips pulled up. She rubbed the sides of her belly.

I stared at her.

"It was a joke, Tim." She rolled her eyes. She nodded toward the truck. "What's going on?"

I shrugged. "I could use a ride to a gas station." I rubbed the back of my neck as I looked at my truck. "Find a phone and call the ranch."

"I could look at it for you." She walked past me to the trunk of her.

I frowned. "No, that's okay."

"I'm serious." She opened the trunk to her car. "I've got enough to jerry-rig almost anything back together."

"I've so many questions." I peered over her shoulder. Bottles of motor oil, antifreeze, and hydraulic fluid were lined up in crates along with several various sized toolboxes.

"Well, cowboy, you're in luck. I'm a certified mechanic." She tucked a strand of hair behind her ear.

"A mechanic? I'd never imagined it."

"I needed a job I can do anywhere." She shrugged and pulled out a toolbox. "I grew up in Uncle Ernie's shop watching him work on cars."

"Why?" I took the toolbox she handed me as she reached for another. "You could've been a nurse or a teacher or..."

"Something more girlie?" She planted her free hand on her hip, challenging me.

"Um..."

She raised an eyebrow.

"Um...I guess. But that's not what I meant."

"Then, tell me, Mr. Kisment. What did you mean?" She turned to my truck.

"Just that I'd never met a woman mechanic before." I followed her.

"Ding-ding, we have a winner." She put her hands on the frame and leaned into the engine. Her belly pressed against the metal of the truck. She maneuvered herself sideways to see further in. "Give me one second." She studied the engine.

A mechanic and pregnant. What had happened to her since we said goodbye after high school? Was there a man in the picture? Or was she in trouble? The sports car was well taken care of but not a new vehicle. She was dressed nice in a flowing dress that hid some of her belly with sandals. What was she doing here in the middle of nowhere in Texas?

She reached for a rag in her toolbox and wiped her hands. "Not the end of the world. I can get it up and running so you can make it home. But it will need to be fixed proper before heading back out."

"What do you need me to do?"

"I'm glad you asked." She smiled at me. "You get to be my hands. I can't reach that far in or lay on my back on the ground to fix it from underneath." She handed me a wrench. "I'll guide you."

Thirty minutes later, I slid out from under the front of the truck. She helped me up and handed me a rag. Our fingers brushed each other's. Tingles radiated up my arms, aching to draw her in for a hug. She cocked her head to the side. A smile played on her lips.

"Let's see if it runs, before you hug me."

"How did you know?" I slid the key into the ignition.

"You have a look."

"You remembered a look?" I turned the key. The engine roared to life, before settling down to a rough idle. I blew out a sigh of relief while Judy cheered.

"Of course. One doesn't forget their first love."

I stepped toward her. "Can I hug you now?"

She nodded.

My hands found her arms, sliding up to her shoulders. I wrapped my arms around her, bringing her closer to me. She drew close, tucking her head under my chin. Her heart beat hard against her chest as she hugged me back.

In that moment, I was transported back to a time I was eighteen. The last hug she gave me felt like this, right before she broke up with me and said goodbye. I pushed away the feelings. I had no right. As far as I should be concerned, we were two almost strangers.

She patted my back before she drew away. "I'll follow you home to make sure you get there."

The loss of her body heat hurt, and I wanted to bring her closer again. The colts stomped. The trailer rocked with the motion.

"Alright. Will I see you again?"

She lifted a shoulder and twirled a loose strand of hair. "I'm spending Christmas with my aunt and uncle in Sunnydale."

I caught the hand twirling the hair. "Perfect. I'll see you tomorrow." I kissed the back of her hand. "Thank you, Judy. I'd still be stuck here if it wasn't for you."

"You are welcome," she whispered. Her eyes grew dark as she watched my lips. "Looking forward to tomorrow." She slowly drew her hand away.

"It was great to see you."

"I know." She called over her shoulder as she walked to her car.

Chapter Two

Judy

I sank into the driver's seat of my car. My heart raced. The skin where his lips touched burned. The butterflies danced in my stomach. And the baby kicked. I closed my eyes and rested my head against the headrest. All of the feelings I felt for Tim Kisment all those years ago hit me like a freight train. I rubbed the side of my belly. Him of all people to run into on my short visit home. The sultry eyes, his easy smile, his broad shoulders, and the way his lips felt on my hand, I swooned inside. I needed to hold it together. I'd be heading back home to Virginia in a couple of days.

Home. The word chased out the warmth I felt from seeing Tim. It was nothing but a shell of a house outside of an army base. There was no home anymore. A tear rolled down my cheek. Even though it had been months, I still haven't been able to make any decisions on what to do next in my life. My husband, Kaleb, died overseas, serving his country. Now, it was just me and our unborn baby. I dashed the tear away and started my car.

Tim drove passed me and waved. I waited for the trailer to clear my front bumper before following him.

The hour drive to the Kisment Ranch, the Rocking K, passed slowly. My thoughts and emotions swung from the happy meeting with Tim, to the excitement of seeing my aunt and uncle, to the dread of heading back "home" at the end of my trip.

I honked as Tim pulled into his driveway. He waved and I waved back. Hopefully, he'd come to visit tomorrow. I touched the gas. The car jumped forward as I drove the last few miles to town.

The city limits of Sunnydale came into view a few minutes later. Everything looked the same from the last time I was here. The cattle sale barn and veterinary clinic were packed with trucks and trailers. I pulled to a stop at the four-way stop sign. The ice cream shop had its lights on. A family was at the counter buying soft serve ice cream cones. Across the street, my Uncle Ernie pumped gas into a station wagon. He waved as I pulled into the gas station parking lot. I drove around the building to park in the back.

I slid out of my car and stretched. It was a long ride from Virginia. It was good to be back. The baby kicked in my belly, seemingly to agree. I placed a hand on my side to quiet the kicking.

The back door to the gas station burst open as my Aunt Sally ran out.

"Oh dear, I'm so glad you made it." She wrapped me in a hug. "It's been too long."

I hugged her back. "It has."

She pulled back. "How's the baby doing?" Her hands fell to the sides of my belly. The baby gave a little kick. "Oh, it's an active one!"

I nodded. "According to the doctors, everything is right on schedule."

"How much longer?"

"About three weeks." I bent over to grab my bag.

"I'll get that." She urged me to the side. "Why don't we go in and have a nice cup of tea?"

"That does sound nice." I placed my hand on my lower back. "Everything aches."

"It will, honey. And it won't get better once the baby comes." She clicked her tongue. "Nor will you sleep again."

"I'd love a good night's sleep."

She shook her head. "Are you sure we can't talk you into staying here? It's not easy raising a baby by yourself."

"We've been over this," I sighed. "I've got to figure out what I want to do next. Whether that is staying in Virginia or moving back here or something else. I don't know what I want."

She opened the back door and ushered me inside. "Well, no need to worry about all of it right now. Just think about the baby."

The gas station had a small garage attached to the back where Uncle Ernie changed oil and rotated tires for people. The lift sat empty. An old radio played jazz in the background. Aunt Sally bustled around the empty garage to the little office. She put a tea pot on a hot plate in the corner.

"How was your trip?" She pulled two chipped mugs from the cupboard, handing me one.

I spun the cup around in my hands. The paint was chipped and faded in areas. "The same mugs as always."

She smiled and took out two teabags. "They work."

"The trip was good. I had to stop a lot more than I wanted." I sank into the rickety chair by the window.

"I expect that. A cross country trip pregnant. Not in my day." She poured the boiling water over the teabags.

I blew at the steaming mug. "I ran into Tim Kisment on the way into town."

"That was fast." She chuckled. "And…" She leaned closer to me. A small smile played on her lips.

"And. What?"

"Any old feelings?" She raised an eyebrow at me.

My cheeks heated under her gaze. I ran my finger around the rim of the mug before swirling the tea. "He said something about meeting tomorrow."

"He's going to wait until tomorrow?" She leaned back in her chair.

"That's what he said."

She sipped her tea. "I bet you that he'll be by tonight."

"Aunt Sally, we aren't teenagers anymore," I scoffed.

"Girl, I doubt his feelings for you have changed since then. The ladies at church gossip that he hasn't dated in years."

My mouth snapped shut. Was it possible that he still had feelings for me? It had been ten years. Things changed. But on the other hand, all the old feelings I had for Tim flooded to the surface after just a few minutes.

Aunt Sally grinned. "I guess we'll see. Won't we?"

Later that evening, Uncle Ernie pushed back from the table and patted the pocket of his buttoned-up shirt. "That was a sure good dinner, Sally." He extracted the cigarettes from his pocket. "I'm going to head out to the porch for my after-dinner smoke." He stuck a cigarette between his lips.

"Want some coffee?" Aunt Sally kissed his cheek as he walked by.

"Would love some." He ran his hand down her arm.

They exchanged a look so full of love that my heart ached at the sight. He took out his cigarette and kissed her on the lips. I sighed. If only I had a relationship like that. It wasn't perfect but they made it work.

Aunt Sally patted her lips where he touched them. A faint smile pulled at the corners and her eyes grew dreamy. Uncle Ernie winked at her before heading down the hall to the front door.

"What would you like for an after-dinner drink?" Aunt Sally turned to me.

"I think..."

"Why, young man! What a surprise to see you this evening!" Uncle Ernie's voice carried from by the front door. "Here to see our Judy?"

"Yes, sir. Like always," Tim said.

Aunt Sally grinned at me. "I told you so." She pointed a finger in the direction of the front door. "He couldn't resist you."

I blushed. "Who would have thought?"

"Look who I found on our front porch?" Uncle Ernie proceeded Tim into the kitchen.

Tim's eyes caught mine. He smiled at me. Heat rushed through me all the way down to my toes. I looked down at my hands, trying not to give away my feelings. The way he looked at me made me feel like I was seventeen again.

"Now, Tim, what do you have planned for our girl this evening?" Uncle Ernie took a cup of coffee from Aunt Sally. His cigarette forgotten behind his ear.

"I thought..." Tim started.

"What's this nonsense, Ernie. They are adults and can do whatever they want." Aunt Sally pushed a cup of joe into Tim's hands.

"Thank you, Sally." He sipped the hot coffee. "I was wondering if you'd like to get a drink?" He directed the words to me.

I rubbed my hand over my belly. "Um, well, I can't really do alcohol or too much caffeine."

"I thought more of catching up than drinking." His eyes held mine. Emotions churned below the surface dragging me to him.

What was it about Tim? We had been sweethearts ten years ago. Surely time would've dimmed the desire. But I guess not.

"I don't see why not." I slowly stood from the table.

Tim crossed the kitchen with long strides to end by my side. Placing his hand under my elbow, he helped me to my feet. His other hand strayed to my lower back. His touch sent my blood racing and my heart pounding. His breath danced over my skin, causing tingles. I became acutely aware of his closeness and masculinity. My body wanted to curl into his, allow him to take care of everything.

Aunt Sally and Uncle Ernie shared a look. They stepped closer together. Uncle Ernie slipped an arm around Aunt Sally's shoulders. She smiled at me and mouthed; *I told you so.*

"Let's get out of here. Bye, Aunt and Uncle," I called over my shoulder.

"Don't get into too much trouble." Uncle Ernie chuckled at his own joke.

I rolled my eyes at him, and he laughed even harder.

"I'll take good care of her, sir," Tim said as we left the kitchen.

Tim's truck sat in front of the house. He helped me into the passenger side before climbing into the driver's seat. I slid over on the bench seat so that I could be close to him, just like old times.

Tim turned the key and the truck started with a roar. He looked over at me and smiled. Butterflies rushed into my stomach. His smile still warmed every inch of me.

"Are we really going out for a drink?" I placed a hand on my ballooning belly.

"I was thinking somewhere more private than the bar." He turned onto the highway that headed out to town.

"As long as there is somewhere comfortable to sit." I wiggled in my seat. "I'm game for anything."

"Um..." He frowned and cast me a sideways look. "I hadn't thought of that. Change of plans." He slapped on the blinker.

The truck tires screeched as he swung a U turn. I gripped his arm to keep my balance. Touching him flared up dormant emotions. Ones that I forgot I had.

"I was going to take you to our spot by the river." He grinned sheepishly. "But I don't think that you'll find that the most comfortable."

"Probably not. I don't think I can get down on the ground or up once I'm down."

"So, we'll go to the 'Make-out point.'" His cheeks pinked in the dim light of the cab.

"I've never been there. Have you?" A flare of jealousy spike in my chest. What if he said yes and went there with another woman? Why did it matter to me? I was pregnant with another man's baby.

He shook his head. "No. I don't date." His fingers gripped the steering wheel tightly.

"Why not?" I regretted the words as soon as they left my lips.

He shrugged. "When you had the best thing in the world, why try to replace it?" He kept his eyes firmly on the road.

My gaze dropped to my hands. I twisted them together. "I never meant..."

"I know. It is my problem." His hand left the steering wheel, covering mine. "We are here."

The truck swung into the empty parking lot of a state park. Tim parked the truck at the end of the blacktop, overlooking the countryside. Hiking trails ran into the wilderness. A sign at the trail head reminded people not to litter and to stay on the trail. I shivered a little and wrapped my arms around myself.

Tim cranked the knobs on the dash until heat blasted from the vents. He unbuckled his seat belt and reached behind the seat. He pulled out an old blanket, a couple bottles of water, and plate of homemade brownies. He wrapped the blanket over my shoulders and set the plate between us.

"From my mother." He unwrapped the plate.

"She makes the best brownies." I reached for one on the edge and slid it off the plate. I took a big bite. Chocolate and caramel oozed over the edges. "I needed this hit of chocolate." I closed my eyes and savored the brownie.

"Don't you have chocolate brownies wherever you are?" Tim took a chunk of one piece and plopped it into his mouth.

"Virginia. And no." I swallowed. "I don't have anyone there to make me brownies."

He nodded and reached for another chunk.

I sipped my water before getting another brownie.

"So..." He cleared his throat. "What brings you to Sunnydale?"

"I didn't want to spend Christmas alone. Aunt Sally and Uncle Ernie have been begging me to come home since..." I gazed out the windshield. Tiny stars sparkled in the navy sky.

"Since?" Tim prompted.

"Since my husband died." I bit my lower lip, throwing a glance at him.

"I'm sorry. I didn't know." His hand covered mine. "Are you okay?"

I snorted. "Okay is a relative term. I'll survive." A tear arched down my cheek. I dashed it away with my free hand. "He loved being a solider and he died doing what he loved." I sniffed. "The ultimate sacrifice for our great country."

Tim squeezed my hand.

"It's been seven months. Some days are harder than others."

"Did he know about the baby?" His voice gentle.

"No." I squeezed my eyes shut picturing that day. "It's so vivid. The day I found out. I'd been to the doctor. I was so excited. A child. I wrote him a letter as soon as I got home." Tears escaped from the corners of my eyes. "I was about to run to the post office when a knock sounded at my door."

Tim scooted closer to me, his arm wrapping around my shoulders.

"There they were. I'm sure I shocked them. They told me the news and I fainted." I dabbed at the tears. "I've never fainted in my life."

"How awful. What about his family?"

I shook my head again. "He was a single child and his parents died when he was in high school. There is no one."

"Almost like you."

"I have Aunt Sally and Uncle Ernie, at least." My gaze settled on Tim. A range of emotions marched across his face. "What do you think of my story?"

He swallowed. "I think you are incredibly strong and brave. You can need people though. It's not a weakness."

"I don't have a lot of trustworthy people in my life."

"You have me."

That was true. His eyes sucked me in. He has always been there for me, at least in the past.

"How about you? What have you been up to?" I picked a small chunk of chocolate left on the plate.

Another car pulled into the lot. Its headlights flashed through the back window of Tim's truck before it drove to the opposite end.

He sat back and ran his fingers through his hair. "I'm studying to be a pastor. I'm in my last year of seminary school right now."

"Really? I'd never guess."

"I didn't know what I wanted to do after college, so I came home to ranch." His gaze moved to the scenery beyond the hood of the truck. "Then one day, Pastor John was sick and I ended up in the pulpit doing the sermon." He laughed. "I don't know how that happened, but it was a sign." He shrugged. "So, I went back to school and now here I am."

I studied him. Was he the same boy I fell in love with all those years ago? That Tim was happiest on horseback, and I never figured he would leave the ranch.

"What does that mean for the ranch?" I cocked my head to the side.

"I'm still working it with Father. I figured I'd ranch during the week and preach on the weekends." He shrugged. "You remember that Pastor John is a carpenter?"

"I remember now that you say that."

"Our church can't afford to pay a full-time wage, and it makes us more relatable." He grinned at me. "At least that is what Pastor John says."

I rubbed my belly and shifted in my seat. My back and feet hurt, even sitting in his truck was uncomfortable. Tim's gaze rested on me. Heat rose in my cheeks.

"It's not comfortable being pregnant."

Chapter Three

Tim

I watched Judy squirm next me. First, she shifted from one side to another. Then, she tucked her legs under her. She would rub her belly, place a hand on her back, or try to squeeze her calves.

"It's not comfortable being pregnant," she said. She moved to set her feet on the floor.

I caught one ankle. "Why don't you lean against the door, and I can rub your feet?"

She frowned. Cute little lines forming between her brows.

"That's if you would like that?" Maybe I was too forward.

"No, that sounds wonderful, if you are serious."

I grabbed the other foot and set them both across my lap as she scooted to rest her back against the door. "My sister always wanted her feet rubbed when she was pregnant." I took off her tennis shoes and socks.

"I haven't had any sort of massage. The women in my pregnancy group all rave about them. But you know, I'm alone." She tilted her head back and closed her eyes.

I ran my hands up and down her calves, massaging the muscle before working the tension from her feet. All the feeling I felt for her all those years ago fought to the surface. I wanted to protect her and the baby. I wanted to give them a home. And most of all I wanted Judy to love me back.

The night we broke up was one of the hardest days of my life. I wasn't sure what to do. I lost my best friend and my soulmate all at the same time. It changed my world forever. That wasn't how I had expected the night to go. A sigh escaped and I closed my eyes blocking out the memory.

"That's a big sigh." Judy's eyes searched my face. "If my feet are so bad, you don't have to do that."

"It's not that." The corner of my lips pulled up a bit. "I was thinking about the night we broke up."

"Oh." Her eyes grew sad. "I am sorry." She chewed on her lower lip. "I think that I disrupted whatever plans you had for the evening."

"You did." I concentrated on her foot.

"It was for the best," she said softly. Her hand rested on my arm.

"Was it?"

Silence filled the space of the cab at my words. Her hand slid from my arm. She started to pull her foot away. I caught it and held. When I looked up, she had tears in her eyes. Her lips turned to a sad small smile.

"It was. Would you have gone to be a pastor? I wouldn't have the baby." She ran her hand over her belly. "We weren't ready to be married, Tim. I needed to see the world."

"You knew? That I bought a ring?"

"Everyone knew. The moment you told your cousin the whole town knew." She sighed. "I'm sorry that I broke your heart. Could you forgive me?"

I gently squeezed her foot. "Of course."

It didn't matter anymore. She was here. She needed me, if only I could get her to see that before she left.

"How long are you staying in town, again?"

"I leave the day after Christmas to head home."

I set her feet down and she scooted back to me. I wrapped an arm around her, drawing her close. Her perfume filled my nostrils. She rested her head on my shoulder. Christmas Eve was the day after tomorrow. I had three days to get her to fall back in love with me.

"That was great. Thank you," she said.

"Anytime," I murmured into her hair.

I couldn't lose her again. No, I was going to do everything in my power to re-ignite the flame between us. I just had to figure out how. That was tomorrow's problem.

She snuggled closer to me. "What a great night."

"It sure is." I wasn't going to let her go, again.

Eventually, the other car left the parking lot. Judy fell asleep against my shoulder. I didn't want to wake her up, but it was getting late. Slowly, I shifted until the key was in the ignition. With a twist, the engine rumbled to life. She bolted up right. Her eyes wide.

"I'm awake."

I chuckled. "It's fine. It's late and I should get you home."

She yawned and stretched before buckling her seatbelt. "You're probably right." She leaned back against me. "You don't mind?"

"Not at all." My fingers intertwined with hers.

"I'm so tired." Her eyelids fluttered and she was asleep before we hit the highway.

I nudged her shoulder a few minutes later. "Judy, wake up. You're home."

She sat up blinking and looking around. The front porch lights were on, waiting for her. A few other lights in the house shone into the black night. She unbuckled her seatbelt and gave me a sad smile.

"My first visit to 'Make out point' and I didn't even get kissed," she said.

"Well, I can change that if you want." I glanced at her out of the corner of my eye as I unbuckled my seatbelt.

Her mouth formed an O. She blinked. "I think that I'd like that very much."

I leaned toward her. My hand cupped the back on her neck and my other hand brushed the stray hair from her cheek. Our eyes locked. My chest tightened as my heart pounded against my ribs. How did this woman make me feel this way? Breathing was hard. I licked my lips. Her eyes went to them and back to my eyes.

"I'd like to," my voice came out deep and gravelly.

She leaned closer. Her eyelids fluttered closed. Her hand pressed against my knee, searing her touch into my skin. Our breath mingled in the cab of my truck. An inch closer. My hand slid to her back.

The porch light flickered off, darkening the truck. Then, it turned back on, dousing the moment in reality.

Judy pulled away. Disappointment clouded her eyes. "That's my cue," she said ruefully. "I'm probably passed curfew. Even though, I'm a grown woman." She rolled her eyes toward the house. "Some things never change."

I sighed. "Come on. I'll walk you to the door."

Back over in the driver's seat, I opened the door and stepped out. The Texas night air was cool and brisk. Not a cloud covered the bright stars. A car backfired a couple blocks away. Christmas music played from one of the neighboring houses. I opened the truck door for Judy and held her hand as she wiggled her way off the seat and onto the ground. Her hand felt perfect in mine. I clasped it as we ambled up the drive.

"Everything alright?" My brows creased into a frown as I watched her free hand make circles on the side of her belly.

"Yes, the kid is just active at night." She sucked in a breath. "It is very strong with the kicks."

"Anything I can do?"

"No, let's keep walking. That sometimes help."

I assisted her up the steps to the front porch. She turned to me, and I reached for her other hand. I squeezed them tightly, not wanting to let her go.

"Judy," I hesitated. "Can I see you tomorrow?" I held my breath, hoping the answer was yes.

She nodded. "I'm looking forward to it."

She leaned into me and lightly pressed her lips to mine. I wanted to wrap her in my arms and hold her against my heart. I wanted the kiss to last. She pulled away after a moment, leaving me cold and wanting more.

"I better go," she whispered, taking a little piece of my heart with her as she went into the house.

The door closed behind her. The kiss lingered on my lips. Her nearness flamed my love for her from a smoldering ember to a flame.

"Keep at it, son." A match struck and a little flame appeared at the side of the house. Ernie lit his cigarette with the burning match.

My eyes adjusted to the darkness. He sat in a chair out of the circle of porch light. A coffee cup sat next to him.

"I plan on it, sir."

He waved the cigarette at me. "Believe me. We are rooting for you to win back her heart."

"You are? What about the porch light?" I stepped off the porch toward him.

He chuckled. "Builds suspense, I guess. That's Sally's department."

I shook my head. "I'll be seeing you tomorrow."

"Come by around noon."

"Can do. Thank you, sir."

Chapter Four

Judy

December 23

Uncle Ernie leaned back in his chair and patted his belly. "You out did yourself again, Sally. Lunch was delicious." He pressed a kiss her to cheek as she reached over his shoulder for his plate.

She blushed, lightly patting his shoulder. "It was just grilled cheese."

I smiled to myself. They were such a cute couple. The love in this house settled my spirit. I needed to come home. Being by myself, I was lost in the loneliness of my house and life. I could feel my soul healing with Aunt and Uncle's love. I rubbed a hand over my abdomen. The baby kicked where my hand touched.

"Judy, you should go get dressed," Aunt Sally picked up my plate where my sandwich sat half eaten.

"Why?" I looked down at my flannel pajamas. "These are comfortable. Tim would call first before he came over."

Uncle Ernie and Aunt Sally shared a look. I narrowed my eyes at them. They were hiding something.

"What is going on?" I pointed my finger at them.

Aunt Sally shrugged. "I think Tim will be here shortly. Go put on something cute."

I frowned. "How do you know that? And something cute? My belly looks like I swallowed a beach ball."

"Oh, honey, no one thinks that." Aunt Sally ran her hand down the length of my hair. "You look gorgeous, but you better get dressed."

The doorbell rang.

"I bet that's Tim." Uncle Ernie got up from his chair. "I'll go distract him."

I sighed and shook my head at them. "Sometimes, you two meddle too much." I pushed myself back from the table. "Do you know where we are going?

"He said something about going to the Riverwalk," Aunt Sally said.

"Give me about ten minutes to find something appropriate." I stood up.

Uncle Ernie opened the front door. "Come in, Tim. Our girl is getting ready." Their voices faded as they moved into the living room.

Aunt Sally poured three mugs of coffee, placing them on a tray. "We'll keep him entertained until you are ready."

I placed a hand on her arm. "Why didn't you tell me he was coming?"

"Oh, honey, I didn't want you to spend your time over analyzing it. I just wanted you to enjoy the moment." She smiled at me. "You've been a shadow of yourself since the funeral." She picked up the tray and pushed through the kitchen door. It silently swung closed behind her.

I shuffled in the other direction toward the stairs. She was right. I had been living in my grief for months. I rubbed my belly. Was I even enjoying the pregnancy, like my friends did? I made the excuse that they were all married and had doting husbands. I worked to support myself. I was alone. Well, not anymore. Once the baby came, there would be another person in my life.

Ten minutes later, I walked into the living room. Tim stood up the moment he saw me. His coffee sloshed over the edge of his mug, spilling onto the coffee table. Aunt Sally discreetly slid a napkin under his mug to catch the drops. His mouth opened and closed.

"What do you think?" I slowly spun in a circle. The full-length skirt billowed out around me.

"You look great." His eyes followed me into the room. They grew darker as his pupils dilated.

Aunt Sally and Uncle Ernie shared a smile before slipping from the room.

He extended his hand to clasp mine. His callused hands engulfed mine. He pulled me closer. His lips tugged up at the corners.

"It was worth the wait." His voice deepened. He took a step closer to me. Only a couple of inches separated me from him. "Do you mind if I kiss you before we go out?"

My heart leaped and my pulse pounded in my ears. "A kiss would be nice." My voice squeaked.

He leaned across the remaining inches. His lips descended, gently putting pressure on mine. His hands gripped my forearms. Electricity radiated out from his touch. My knees buckled as the kiss swept me away. His fingers squeezed into my arms, stabilizing me. He broke the kiss after a few seconds and set me back on my heels. Emotions swirled in his eyes. My breath came in short bursts.

"That's dangerous to do first thing," he whispered against my skin.

I tried to control my racing thoughts. I licked my lips, and his gaze fell to them. He took another step back.

"I agree. We might not make it out of the living room." My cheeks burned. "I'm sure Aunt and Uncle are behind the door, listening to us."

He raised an eyebrow and reached for his cowboy hat on the couch. "Do you want to give them something to talk about while we are gone?" He placed it on his head.

"Not really." My gaze drank in the sight of him. His cowboy hat completed the look of jeans, a pressed western shirt, silver belt buckle, and polished cowboy boots. "I forgot how much I like cowboys."

He chuckled and slipped my hand in the crook of his elbow. "Well, my lady, let this cowboy show you what else you might've forgotten."

"Sounds like fun." I allowed him to lead me from the room.

The thirty-minute drive to San Antonio passed quickly as we talked about our lives since high school, caught up on friends, and discussed our tastes in music. Tim maneuvered his truck through San Antonio to the Riverwalk and parked in a public parking lot. He searched in the glove compartment for spare change and came out with a handful.

"I'll feed the meter and be right back." He slipped from the truck and inserted coins into the meter.

I flipped down the visor and checked my make-up. The ride to San Antonio was reminiscent of the many trips to the city we made as teenagers. The conversation flowed and we fell back into our old patterns. I touched up my lipstick. Was I a fool to leave him all those years ago? Did he hold it against me?

He jogged to my side of the truck and opened the door. He held out his hand to me. "Are you ready?"

"Sure am." I placed my hand into his and slid down from the seat. My balance was thrown off by my belly. When my feet hit the ground, I tipped forward. Right into his chest. His arms wrapped around me, holding me tight to him. His heart beat hard against my hands. I tilted my head up to meet his gaze.

"Are you alright?" His voice deep and gravelly.

I smiled at him. "The baby changes my center of gravity. I'm clumsier than normal."

He kissed the top of my head before setting on my feet. "I'll be sure to catch you whenever you need it."

My cheeks heated under his gaze. What did he mean by that? "I appreciate it. Where are we heading to first?"

His fingers entwined with mine. "We are going to the Alamo Plaza. It's a few blocks away."

He led me toward the Plaza. As we got closer, the crowds on the sidewalk got thicker. Families chased little children around. Couples walked arm in arm, sharing stolen glances. People carried bags from the stores full of last-minute Christmas presents. I squeezed his hand. Tim glanced at me and smiled.

The trees were covered in twinkling Christmas lights and more strands were strung over the sidewalks. The hotels had tall green Christmas trees in their front windows covered in little lights and glass ornaments. Little roadside booths sold hot chocolate and kettle corn.

"This is magical." I slowly turned around taking in the plaza.

"I thought you would like it."

"It's been years since I've been here. So much has changed."

He caught my hand back up. "Well, where do you want to start? Shopping, the Riverwalk, or something else?"

"Could we just walk around a bit?" The lights and the sights drew my attention. I didn't need to shop. It was only Uncle Ernie and Aunt Sally for Christmas. I already had their gifts.

"Sounds like a plan." He gently tugged on my arm to guide me in the direction of the store fronts. "Let's start here and make our way around."

We walked and window shopped for an hour before my body started to ache. My feet hurt and my lower back screamed at me.

"Do you mind if we sit down for a while?" I rubbed at my lower back, hoping to ease the pain.

"Let's go to the Crockett Hotel. We can get something to drink and sit down on their couches for a bit."

"How do you know all of this?" I smiled at him. "A cowboy going to fancy places downtown?" I squeezed his hand.

He winked at me as we climbed the stone steps. "A cowboy's got to take a break from cowboying sometimes. I like to come down here to study in my free time."

He opened the door and a blast of heat hit me square in the face. He dropped me off at a cluster of plush leather couches before he went to order our drinks. I sunk into the couch and the leather squeaked pleasantly under my weight. I sighed, propped my sore feet on a little table, and rested my head back against the cool leather. I closed my eyes for a moment, hoping to ease the pain and tension in my body. The baby wiggled a bit before settling down. My hand went to my belly where the baby bumped lightly against my touch. A smile played on my lips.

"Here you go." Tim came back. "Hot chocolate for you. I had them add extra whip cream."

"Sounds perfect." I took the mug from him and put it to my lips. The whip cream was fluffy and sweet while the hot chocolate had undertones of dark chocolate and cinnamon. "This is delicious." I set the cup down.

Tim reached across the short table that separated us. His hand paused at the corner of my mouth. His eyes grew dark with passion as his index finger wiped the whipped cream from the corner of my mouth. His touch set my nerves on fire. Heat rushed to the spot his finger touched and my cheeks flamed. He withdrew his hand, never breaking my gaze. He popped his finger into his mouth and licked the whipped cream. "It is good."

My body wanted to launch itself across the table and into his arms. I wanted to beg him to kiss me and hold me forever. My heart raced at the image and my cheeks grew hotter.

"Are you alright?" Tim asked.

I blinked. I was in a coffee shop with a man I hadn't seen in years. I couldn't possibly be having fantasies about him. "Just thinking," I muttered.

"About?" His eyes twinkled in a mischievous way that said he knew what I had been thinking.

I tucked a loose strand behind my ear. "I've been thinking that today has been really nice." I inched myself back on the cushion, anything to put some distance between us.

"I hear a but coming." His eyes held mine, coaxing an answer.

Chapter Five

Tim

She seemed to steel herself. She sat up straighter and rested her feet on the floor. She crossed her arms over the top of her rounded belly. She never looked more beautiful than at that moment. I waited on the rest of her thought.

She bowed her head and twisted her hands together on the top of her belly. "But this can't happen between us."

My heart sank at her words. Did she not feel the same thing that I felt? The world seemed to right itself when I was with her. Time stood still. I removed the cowboy hat from my head and ran my fingers through my hair.

"Why is that?"

Her cute little lips opened and closed for a moment. Her eyes darted around the room until they settled back on me. "I'm pregnant with someone else's baby."

I shrugged. "If we were together, I'd love the baby as if he or she was mine. I've always wanted a family."

She frowned. "Most men don't feel that way."

"Most men haven't waited for their soulmates to waltz back into their lives. Baby or not," I leaned forward. "Judy, I'm serious about this."

"So am I. This is all too fast. I've only got here and ran right into you."

"Don't you think it was God's plan?" I set my coffee down and drew closer to her. Our hands were inches away from each other. I wanted to touch her and ease her worries.

"Maybe. But what if this isn't real? What if we are moving too fast? We both have changed since we were in high school." Her eyes darted around the room again. They caught on the barista mixing coffee before coming back to me.

"Judy," I dropped my voice. She leaned closer to catch my words. "Are you afraid of forgetting him?"

She sucked in her breath through her front teeth as she drew away from me. I cringed. Maybe not the right way to go about this. I waited.

She stared down at her ring finger and traced the faint indent that encircled the base of the finger. "Maybe," she said softly. "Maybe, if I let myself love you, it would be like he never existed." Her voice caught. She bit her lower lip between her teeth as her eyes met mine.

I nodded. "Would he want you to not love again?" My breath caught as I waited for her answer.

She touched her ring finger again as she chewed on her lip. "I don't know. We never talked about it." She sucked in a breath and rubbed a spot on her belly. "He wouldn't want the baby to grow up without a dad...No, he wouldn't want me to be alone." Her eyes fluttered to mine. "Are you sure you want to go down this path? It's not just me anymore. In a few weeks, there will be a baby and all that goes with it."

I caught her hand in between mine. I wanted to shout from the rooftops that I'd love a chance to fall back into love with her. Instead, I gazed deep in her eyes. "Judy, give me a chance while you are home. Let's enjoy each other and see where it takes us. How does that sound?"

Her hand made large circles on the side of her belly. Her shirt seemed to stretch a little more and she cringed. "Baby kicking." She smiled a little bit. "I think that is fair. I'm only here for a few days before I head back to Virginia. What are we going to do next?"

I glanced through the big windows. A horse drawn carriage pulled up outside. The horse lowered his head and blew out through his nose. The driver climbed down, patted the horse on the head, and gave him a carrot. The horse bumped the driver's shoulder with his nose.

"I was going to take you to the Riverwalk, but let's take the carriage." I stood up and offered my hand to her.

She placed her dainty hand in mine and levered herself against me to pull herself to her feet. "That sounds wonderful. My feet are killing me."

I tucked her hand in the crook of my elbow. "Carriage ride it is."

We walked out of the hotel and across the pavement to where the horse and carriage stood waiting. The driver pulled out a small step stool. He set it next to the entrance to the carriage and assisted Judy inside.

He handed her a blanket and a small pillow. "My daughter is having her first in a few weeks. These will help with the ride."

"Thank you." Judy sighed as she placed the pillow at the small of her back. "This is heavenly." I placed the blanket over her knees.

"Enjoy the ride, miss." He tipped his hat to her and climbed on to the carriage seat. With a flick of his wrist and a cluck, the horse pulled against the harness until the carriage rolled forward. The driver guided the horse out into traffic.

I wrapped my arm around Judy's shoulders, tucking her against my side. She rested her head on my shoulder and sighed.

The carriage wheels creaked as they rolled over the paved road. The horse's horseshoes clanged against loose rocks. We swayed with the movement of the carriage as it drove up and down streets.

"Thank you," Judy whispered in my ear.

"For what." I placed a kiss on her forehead.

"For not making me walk another step."

I smiled into her hair. If she would let me, I would take care of her for the rest of her life. Now, how was I going to convince her to let me? I didn't know, but I needed to figure it out before she left after Christmas.

The carriage ride went on for thirty minutes before it ended back at the hotel. I paid the driver and he handed us two carrots to give the horse. Judy was rubbing the horse's forehead and kissed its nose when the driver cleared his throat.

"Miss, good luck with everything." He tipped his hat to her.

She smiled at him and kissed the horse's nose one more time.

He leaned down to talk to me. "Take good care of that one."

I nodded. "I am trying."

He winked. "You are doing good so far."

Another set of customers approached for a ride. I took Judy's hand and led her a few feet away. "I was hoping to take you out for dinner tonight."

She sighed, placing a hand at the small of her back. She stretched back and groaned. "I'd love it, but I'm beat. Can I take a raincheck?"

"Sure, let's get you home."

We walked the few blocks to the public parking lot where my truck sat. A station wagon was parked next to my truck. The hood was up, and a couple was yelling at each other over the nose of the vehicle. A small boy sat in the back seat crying while a baby sucked her thumb.

"It's all your fault!" The woman shouted at the man, "I told you to turn off the lights."

"You don't have to yell. I know it's my fault." He glared right back at her.

We stopped at the tailgate of my truck as the fuming continued. Judy frowned when she saw the kids and pulled away from me. She slowly made her way up to the front of the station wagon. As the couple argued, she investigated the engine.

"Excuse me," she interrupted them.

They startled and turned to look at her with their mouths open.

"I'm a mechanic and I think I can help you."

"The battery is dead. He left the lights on." The woman crossed her arms over her chest.

"It was an honest mistake," he spat back at her.

"Anyway." Judy rolled her eyes. "I can fix this if you want."

"That would be great." The woman glanced in the backseat of the car. "We are so far from home. We don't know what to do."

"Not a problem." Judy smiled at them. Turning to me, she said, "I need a few rags and jumper cables."

"Yes ma'am. Coming right up." I opened the tailgate of my truck and pulled out what she needed.

She tucked a rag into the back of her waistband and bent over the front of the station wagon. She reached into the engine.

"I see. Well, this might be the problem. Let me check this," she muttered to herself.

The family clustered around her. The woman held the sleeping baby, and the man gripped the little boy's hand. They peered over her shoulder as she worked. I leaned against the front bumper of my truck and crossed my arms against my chest. Her face lit up with excitement the more she inspected the car. I imagined her in a mechanic's jumpsuit with grease stains on her cheeks and her eyes passionate about the internal combustion engine of the automotive. My lips twitched into a grin. She was really cute.

"Ha! Got it." She pulled the rag out of her waist band and stuck it further into the engine. After a few minutes, she straightened and turned around to the couple. "Your battery terminals are corroded which means the battery didn't charge while you drove."

The couple frowned at her.

"So, when you left the lights on, it drained what's left of your battery." She wiped her hands on the rag and picked up the jumper cables. "I cleaned off the terminals as best as I could. We'll give you a jump, but you are going to want to get it checked out when you get home."

I popped the hood on my truck. Judy attached the cables to the dead battery and handed me the other end. I attached them to my battery and started my truck. It rumbled to life and then settled down for a rough idle. Judy raised her eyebrows at me. I shrugged. After a few minutes, the man twisted the key in the ignition. The station wagon sputtered and spat. He gave it a little gas before the engine caught. The woman beamed and the little boy ran around her, jumping up and down with excitement. The woman hugged Judy. Tears streamed down her face.

"Thank you so much! I wasn't sure how we were going to get home," she said.

Judy blushed. The pink color tinged her cheeks and the tips of her ears. My heart filled with love at how adorable she was. My girl was a talented mechanic and a sweet person.

"Not a problem." Judy hugged the woman back. "I'm glad I could fix it." She undid the jumper cables and slammed the hood.

"What do we owe you?" The man pulled out his wallet. The leather bifold was thin.

Judy shook her head and held out her hands. "No money, please."

I climbed down from my truck and stood next to her. Wrapping my arm around her, I pressed a kiss to her hairline. Judy smiled up at me and our gazes locked. The whole world froze so it was just her and I. The lines at the corner of her eyes crinkled as she leaned into me. She slid one hand to her belly while the other squeezed my hand at her shoulder.

"Thank you so much. You two are such an adorable couple. When is your baby due?" The woman shifted her baby to her other arm. The little boy tugged at her arm.

"Mommy," he said in a loud whisper. "I need to..." He crossed his legs.

"Come on, son." His father grabbed his hand and lead him across the street to a public bathroom.

"We aren't a..." I slid my arm from her shoulder and started to step away.

Judy grabbed my hand. "A few weeks." She winked at me.

"Well, enjoy the peace while you can." The woman looked after her husband and little boy. "It will never be the same. Thank you, again." She opened the passenger door and checked on her sleeping baby in the carseat. She settled herself into the passenger seat with a little wave.

I walked Judy to the passenger side and helped her into my truck. Then, I unattached the jumper cables from my vehicle, closed the hood, and threw them in the back of my truck. I climbed into the driver's seat. She had her head rested against the window and her legs propped up on the bench seat.

"Good job today." I backed my truck out of the parking spot.

"All in a day's work," she murmured. Her eyelids grew heavy.

"I thought you were impressive."

A smile played on her lips. Her breathing deepened and her body relaxed.

"I love you, Judy," I murmured under my breath. Silence greeted my words. My girl was sound asleep. If only, she'd believe me when I told her.

Chapter Six

Judy

Day of Christmas Eve, December 24th

The next morning, Tim knocked on our front door. I swung it open. He stood there smiling at me. The sun peaked over the horizon, painting the sky with streaks of blues and pinks. The morning air bit at my cheeks and my breath lingered in little puffs.

I stifled yawned and rubbed at my tired eyes. "You seem chipper this morning."

He shrugged, placing his hand on the doorway. He leaned closer. "I couldn't sleep last night." His voice dropped low and husky. "I was thinking about you."

I blinked. My heart melted a bit. I inched closer to him. "What about?"

His eyes caressed my face. His eyebrows raised. "Our next kiss."

I swallowed. Our next kiss. I thought about that too last night.

"What are you kids up to this morning?" Uncle Ernie's voice pierced the mood, deflating it like a balloon. He appeared in the doorway behind me. I shifted to the side.

Tim straightened up and removed his cowboy hat. "Good morning, sir." He moved his attention to me. "If you are up for it, we can head to the ranch."

"And?"

"I was thinking we could hitch up the team and go for a drive around the place." A little blush colored his neck. "It isn't as good as a sleigh ride through the snow."

I laughed. "No, not in south Texas. I have my fill of snow back in Virginia. It would be nice to see the ranch... If I can get something warm to drink." I really wanted coffee, but pregnant women aren't supposed to have caffeine.

"I have a thermos of hot chocolate in the truck," Tim said.

"That will work."

Uncle Ernie chuckled and patted my shoulder. "Have fun and don't stay out too late. Your Aunt is preparing a feast for Christmas Eve."

Sunnydale passed in a blink of an eye. Before I knew it, we were heading out of town toward the Kisment Ranch, the Rocking K.

"Most of the men have gone home to their families. I'll have to hook up the cart myself, if you don't mind waiting."

"I could help. I'm sure I can at least hold the horses."

"Are you sure? It is a hard job."

I chuckled. "Last time, I was distracted by a handsome cowboy." Back in high school, I was holding the bridles of the team when one of the cowboys threw a bucket of water over Tim. It was hot and he wore a faded T-shirt. It clung to every chiseled muscle he had. I may have loosened my grip on the bridles. One of the horses spooked at the bucket of water. He jumped sideways and broke free. It took us forty-five minutes to catch him, ending our outing in the cart.

"You thought I was handsome." His eyes flickered to me before landing back on the road. Uncertainty colored them.

MY FIRST KISMENT CHRISTMAS

"Yep." I straightened on my side of the seat and lightly punched him in the shoulder. "And still do."

The tips of his ears pinked. He cleared his throat. "There won't be any impromptu showers today."

I shivered. "It's too cold."

His lips quirked into a smile. "That it is."

"Now, you promised hot chocolate?"

He nodded to the stainless-steel thermos resting against the floorboards. "Careful. It'll be hot."

"I need it hot." I rolled the thermos closer to me and picked it up. I poured it into the attached cup and sipped. "This is good."

Before I knew it, we made the turn into the Rocking K ranch. A group of horses stood around a hay bale feeder eating their breakfast. Cows mooed to their calves as they ran around. The herd of cows formed a crooked line. They ambled toward the main barn where a cowboy banged on a feed bucket. A rooster crowed and an engine backfired.

"Things haven't changed too much." I glanced at the old ranch house with the peeling paint and the line of trucks parked at the barn.

Tim shrugged. "We are building a bunkhouse in the back for our single cowboys. We've gotten some new equipment." He angled his truck in line with the others and turned his smile on me. "But most of it is the same. I'll help you out."

He jumped out of his side, slammed the truck door, and jogged to the passenger door. It opened with a squeak. I gripped his offered hand. As it closed around mine, the calluses and rough skin from working outdoors rubbed against mine, sending electricity through me at the touch. My heart pounded in my chest and the baby danced in my belly.

"Judy, welcome to the Rocking K." He supported me as I slid from the seat.

My feet touched the ground. His hands moved to my upper arms, holding me gently. His eyes caught mine. The emotion swirled in them, his lips parted, and his breath ghosted upon my cheeks. I wanted him to wrap me in his arms and hold me tight against his strong chest.

"I would kiss you, but I'm afraid my mother is watching from the window." He nodded toward the house. A curtain fell back into place and a shadow moved behind it.

"Waiting always makes it better." I winked at him.

He stammered and let go of my arms.

"Come on, Tim. Let's go see some horses." I slipped my arm through the crook of his elbow and took a step toward the barn.

The barn doors were opened wide. Dust particles danced in the early morning sun. The smell of hay, horses, and leather filled the air. One cowboy sat against the wall, cleaning his saddle, and whistling a tune. He tipped his hat to us as we walked by. Tim greeted him. Another cowboy threw hay into the stalls. The horses munched happily at it with some snorting and stomping of hooves.

He led me to a couple of stalls in the middle where the two old black Percheron mares stood side by side. They shared their hay through the bars in the stall walls.

"Thelma and Louise." I laughed. "How old are they now?"

Tim lifted the halters from the hooks in front of the stall. "Twenty-two and twenty-three. Father still drives them to rake hay and in parades. Nothing too strenuous for the old girls." He let himself into the stall and slipped a halter over Thelma's ears. He tied her up before doing the same for Louise.

A box in front of each stall held curry combs, brushes, and hoof picks. I picked out a soft brush from Thelma's box. "I always forget how big these two are until I stand next to them." I ran the brush down her silky hair, lifting the dust from her. The black coat shined in no time. She twisted her head around and pressed her nose against my belly. The baby kicked. I laughed.

Tim leaned over the stall wall. His eyes full of emotion. "She knows."

"It seems that way." I rubbed the wide forehead. The intelligent brown eyes blinked at me. She blew out a breath and went back to munching on her hay. The silence grew between us as we brushed down our horses.

Tim let himself into Thelma's stall. He picked up her hooves and cleaned out the dirt and rocks from her hooves. I went outside the stall and sat on a bale of hay.

"Do you like ranching?" I leaned my head against the rough stall walls. My hands cradled the baby within me. My eyes closed as I took in the morning sounds of the barn.

His voice came over my shoulder. "I can't think of anywhere I wished to be."

I opened my eyes to see him leaning over the door, gazing at me intently. My stomach flip-flopped at his expression.

"How about you? Do you love being a mechanic?"

I nodded. "I do. I'm good at it and I love seeing people's reaction when I fix their cars."

A smile played on the corners of his lips. "I like watching you. Your eyes light up when you are figuring out a problem."

Warmth shot through me.

"Do you like living in Virginia?" He turned back to Thelma and rubbed her forehead.

I closed my eyes again. Did I love my home? Did I love being in Virginia? "Not really. It was where the military sent us."

He grunted in response.

"I don't know what I'll do. I don't have any family there. The house is too big, and I never really liked it. I like my job, but that's not a reason to stay."

"What are you going to do when the baby comes?"

I lifted a shoulder. "I have no idea. Aunt Sally said she would come and help for a while. But she is needed here and can't stay forever."

"Would you move back here?" He slid the harness on Thelma and adjusted the buckles. His back still toward me.

Could I move back home and live in my aunt and uncle's house? I wrinkled my nose at that. No, I'd need my own place and job. I had to set a good example for my little one. Tim paused tightening the buckles. His hands rested on the side of the big black horse.

"Maybe. Depends." I rubbed the side of my belly.

Chapter Seven

Tim

"Maybe. Depends."

Those two little words either fanned the little flame within me or snuffed it out completely. What did it depend on? Could I convince her to stay? Was I enough for her to stay here in sleepy little Sunnydale? My hope burned a little brighter. If nothing else, it was an opening for me to sell her on staying in Sunnydale.

I finished with the harness on Thelma and quickly put Louise's harness on. The buckles jingled as I adjusted the harness. I slipped her bridle on over her ears and buckled it.

"Are you ready?" I leaned over the stall door. Louise nudged me in the back, saying she was ready to go.

Judy's eyes fluttered open, and she slid her feet to the hard packed dirt. "Yep, as I am going to be."

"Alright, open the stall doors for us and we're heading out to the hitching rail. The cart is right there."

Judy swung both stall doors open and led the way down the barn aisle. She walked slower today than yesterday. She placed a hand on her lower back as she moved. The horses fell in step behind me. Not in any hurry. They earned the name, "gentle giant".

The barn door was open. The morning sun streamed in, falling on the hard packed dirt. The cowboy cleaning tack set down his bridle and saddle soap.

"I'll help get the cart." He jogged ahead of us. His spurs jingled with every step.

Judy slowly settled on to the bench sitting next to the door. With the cowboy's help, I hooked up both horses in no time. He stood at their heads and held on to their bridles.

"Are you ready?" I helped Judy on to her feet.

"As I'm ever going to be."

We walked the few feet to the cart. I lifted her into the cart and tucked a blanket around her knees. Then, I climbed in, palming the lines. I nodded to the cowboy. He stepped back.

"Come on, ladies." I clicked my tongue. The two Percheron mares stepped out in stride. The harness jingled, chains rattled, the wooden cart groaned, and the gravel crunched under the wooden wheels. I steered them around the barn and down the drive to the gravel road.

Judy leaned into my shoulder and slipped one hand into the crook of my elbow. The other hand held on to the railing around the seat. "The blanket might be overkill."

I shrugged and flapped the lines. The pace increased to a lumbering trot. "I didn't want you to get cold. They can create quite a breeze."

"Where are we going?" Judy's hair flowed around her face. The cart bounced over a few bigger rocks.

"Down the road a bit to the trail that runs around one of our hayfields. It eventually leads back to the barn."

"Sounds like fun." She rested her head on my shoulder.

I transferred the lines to one hand and wrapped my other arm around her, tucking her in close to my side. Right next to my heart. She fit perfectly like she had always belonged there. I needed to convince her to stay next to my heart.

"This is nice," she said.

"It is." I clucked my tongue and flapped the reins at Louise. She slacked in the harness, letting Thelma do most of the pulling. She picked up her pace and leaned into the harness.

We went down the road for two miles. We passed hayfields and open pastures. The dormant grass rustled in the wind. It was peaceful with jangling of the harnesses, creak of the cartwheels, and clopping of the horses' hooves. Judy snuggled in beside me. Her perfume lingered about her. The light floral scent brought me back to our high school days when she first started wearing it.

The entrance to the trail came up quickly.

"Whoa, girls," I said. The two horses slowed to a walk before rolling to a stop. I handed the reins to Judy. Her eyes grew large like Texas when she stared down at the leather straps. "I just need you to hold them, so I can get the gate."

"I can hold the reins alright, but I can't do anything if they want to leave."

I climbed down from the cart. Thelma was resting one hind leg and Louise dozed next to her. "You'll be alright." I walked around the front of the horses, stroking their foreheads. Thelma nudged me. "The next part will be more fun."

A metal gate closed the trail head off from the road. A chain looped around one end held it snug against a post. I lifted the heavy gate up from where it rested in the dirt and wiggled the chain loose from the gate. It swung open, catching on the tufts of tall grass and dirt clods. I pushed it open as far as I could.

"Judy, can you steer the team over here."

"What? You said that I just had to hold the reins." She sat straight up right. The reins draped over the tips of her fingers.

I shrugged and pushed back my cowboy hat. "You do have to do that. I'm sure you can drive anything on wheels. This won't be hard. They are good horses."

She narrowed her eyes at me. "You are such a flatterer, Tim Kisment." She gripped the reins in her palms and sat on edge of the bench seat. "Alright, ladies." The horses flicked their ears at her, standing at attention. "Let's go through the gate." She hesitantly pulled on the rein to turn them and clucked with her tongue.

Thelma and Louise leaned into their harnesses and made the turn through the gate and down the grassy trail. They stopped once the cart was inside the gate. I jerked the cart free from the tall grass and dirt clumps to close it behind us. I climbed into the cart and settled next to Judy.

"See not so hard." I held out my hands to take the reins.

She leaned away and her hands curled around the leather. "I want to drive. That was fun."

I chuckled. "Hooked, are you?"

"Well, as long as the trail isn't too hard." She worried her bottom lip. Her gaze drawn down the trail.

"Nope, it is flat, wide, and mostly straight." I leaned against the back of the seat, resting my arm behind her. "Take up some more slack in the reins. They need to know you are there. If they are draped, they can get caught up in things and it surprises the horses when you pull on them."

She slid her hands down the reins until the slack in them was gone. She glanced over at me. Her eyes full of excitement. Her lips inches from mine. So close. Remnants of the lip gloss she applied this morning glistened in the morning light. They parted and her breath came out in little puff.

"What next?" Her voice shaky and low.

"Next." I swallowed and leaned my shoulders closer to her. "Would be to..."

Louise snorted and Thelma pulled at her bridle. The lines slipped a few inches through Judy's hands. The horses took off at a slow trot. Judy gave a small yelp as she fought to regain her balance on the seat. I reached over caught the lines before they slipped even more from her fingers.

"Easy, Louise. Easy, Thelma." I pulled back on the lines. They slowed to a walk. Thelma chopped at her bit and tossed her head. "Are you alright?"

Judy slid on the seat until she rested against the back rest. One hand clutched the top of the seat, her knuckles white. She rubbed the side of her abdomen with the other hand. "Just startled me and the baby."

"Are you sure?" I scanned her from head to toe.

She nodded. "Give me a few to catch my breath. Then, I want to drive."

"Yes, ma'am," I said. "Come on, girls. Let's move out." I clucked my tongue at them. They picked up a trot.

The trail was level and smooth even with the tall grass growing on either side of it. Their hooves made a muted sound on the soft dirt. The harness jingled and the cart creaked. After a few minutes, Judy straightened in her seat and reached for the lines.

"My turn," she said. Her eyes glittered with excitement.

"You sure about it?" I frowned over at her. Her cheeks were a rosy pink and her eyes sparkled.

"Yes, give them to me." She took the lines from my hands. The horses didn't break stride. "You worry too much."

I rubbed the back of my neck and pulled the brim of my cowboy hat down low. "You've always said that."

"It's as true now as it was then."

A large tree loomed over the path where it curved to go around it. I held my breath. She guided the two draft horses around the tree and back on the straight path. My breath whooshed out in relief.

"See. I got this." She winked at me before turning her attention to the trail. "Do you remember the first time we took these two out for a drive?"

"How could I forget? Father had just bought these two at an auction. He didn't know how they drove." I tipped my hat back to let the morning sun hit my face as the memory of that day washed over me.

"Yep. You handed me the lines and said just hold them." She giggled. "I flopped them across their backs, and they took off."

I laughed. "You looked like a stagecoach driver. The cart skidded around behind them."

"Oh, to be young and carefree." Her voice tinged with a little sadness.

I wrapped my arm around her, hugging her close. "We were lucky no one got hurt or damaged anything."

"I think you were grounded for a month after that." She shifted her weight to the side.

"It was worse than that."

"Really?"

"Yep. Grounded for a month. Had to clean all the stalls twice a day and clean out Mother's chicken coop."

She wrinkled her nose. "Yuck."

For the rest of the drive, we swapped memories of our high school days. The horses jogged along the trail. The sun rose overhead with a warmth that only late December has. After an hour, the trail led back to the ranch. The horses tugged on their bits and trotted faster.

"Here, I'll take them." I took the lines from Judy. "We can't come into the ranch with gravel flying." I smiled at her.

She smiled right back. "What would your parents say to that?"

"Mother wouldn't be happy that a pregnant lady is driving the team. Father will ask if we got into a wreck." I cut a glance at her.

Judy rubbed the side of belly again and shifted her weight around. "They have no faith in me."

"They always thought you were a dare-devil and heartbreaker." The words slipped out before I could stop them. My ears grew hot as the smile melted from her face.

Chapter Eight

Judy

"Tim, I didn't mean to break your heart." I tucked a strand of hair behind my ear. The toe of my shoe had a dirt smudge on it. "I didn't mean for it to be permanent." I caught my lower lip between my teeth. How could I make him understand? "I wanted us to find our own way in the world."

His eyes grew somber. He steered the girls into the middle of the path. My heart broke again, even after all those years. I placed a hand on his arm.

"Can you honestly say that you would be doing what you do right now, if we stayed together?"

The corner of his mouth pulled up into a sad smile. "I'd probably be driving you around in this cart as my wife."

I rolled my eyes at him. "That's not what I meant."

"I know what you meant." He gazed off further down the trail, lost in thought.

"Would you be studying to be a pastor?" I urged gently.

He sighed. "No, probably not. Life would have been different. Doesn't mean that it would have been better or worse."

"True." I shifted my weight. "Are you happy with your life?"

"Yes." He clucked and tapped Louise on the hindquarters. She increased her speed to match Thelma. "What about you? Do you regret leaving?"

"The only thing I regret is breaking your heart." I laced my fingers through his. The leather line running across our palms. "I don't want to break it again."

He placed a kiss at my temple. "Don't worry about it."

I sighed and rested my head on his shoulder. "If I hadn't left, I never would have become a mechanic or traveled as much as I did. And there is this baby." I placed a hand on my belly. The baby kicked against it.

"A child is a gift."

My heart ached at his words. Why did he always have to say the right thing? Why couldn't he be nasty about it? That wasn't fair. Tim was always the one taking care of people, befriending the kid being picked on, and he couldn't help it. "He or she will be. I wish I had told my husband though. I regret that I wasn't able to tell him."

Tim squeezed my hand. "I'm sure he's watching over both of you right now."

A tear squeezed out of my eyelids and rolled down my cheek. "That is beautiful. It makes me feel better."

He squeezed my hands again. He was always understanding and supportive, making him the nicest man I knew. I felt myself falling for him all over again. Maybe this was a mature love. Maybe this one would last. Or maybe, it was the pregnancy hormones kicking in?

The horses turned a last corner. The ranch house and barn came into view. There were fewer trucks parked in front of the barn than there were before. Tim's mother came out of the house with a large thermos and a plate of chocolate chip cookies as we pulled into the yard. She set them down on a bench and grabbed the headstalls of Thelma and Louise.

"I brought hot chocolate and cookies to keep your energy up." She smiled at me. "Do you want to stay for lunch?"

"No, thank you. Aunt Sally is expecting me for lunch." I stifled a yawn. "I might need a nap after all the fresh air.

Tim climbed down from his seat next to me. He extended his hand to help me down. I placed my hand in his. Electricity buzzed at our touch, sending tingles up my arm. My heart raced. Using him as a counterbalance, I stood up. The world seemed to tip and angle. I tipped right along with it. Tim's hands slid under me and caught me against his chest. The world settled on its right axis, leaving me embraced in his arms. His biceps flexed where my fingers dug in for purchase. Our hearts beating as one. Worry clouded his eyes as he slowly set me down on my feet.

"Are you going to be alright?" A cool breeze drifted between us, bringing me back to the moment.

I nodded. "Stood up too fast."

"You gave us both a fright," said his mother. "Dear Judy, how far along are you?"

"I have three weeks left." I leaned on Tim's shoulder to enjoy being near him one more time. His presence did something funny to me where I wanted to be touching him all the time.

"Oh, girl, you aren't going to make three weeks." She shook her head.

"Mother, that's enough." Tim let me go and unhooked the horses from the cart. "Thank you for the hot chocolate and cookies."

She smiled at him and patted his hand when he took the horses from her. "Good to see you, Judy. Looking forward to seeing you at church."

"Thank you for the snacks, Mrs. Kisment." Exhaustion gripped me. I needed a nap and a chance to put my feet up.

The barn was quiet. All the other horses were out, and no cowboys could be seen. Tim led the girls into their stalls and took off their harnesses. I picked up a brush and entered Thelma's stall. She gave a low nicker and placed her nose against my belly. The baby gave a little kick.

"The baby is in there." I stroked her long forehead before running the brush over her sides. The road dust came off in small clouds with the flick of my wrist. Soon, she was shiny black again.

"You looking for a job?" Tim leaned over the stall door. "We could use a good horse brusher around here."

"That's not a real job." I dunked my hand in her water bucket and flung droplets at him. He laughed and ducked into Louise's stall.

"I bet I could beat you to the hot chocolate and cookies." He ran his brush over Louise's back.

"That's not fair. A turtle could probably beat me."

"It would have to be a fast turtle. The one's I've seen move slower than you."

I laughed. "Do you remember the time in high school when we raced on those colts?"

He chuckled. "What were we thinking? Those horses were barely broke, and you just got on and off you went. It wasn't much of a race. It was more of a chase."

"I thought it was fun."

"I'm sure you did. I was worried the colt would dump you. I didn't know how I would explain that to my parents."

I splashed him again with some water. "That's easy. 'Mom and Dad, Judy did something crazy and I was trying to stop her.'"

He flung large cold-water droplets back at me. "I said that a lot. I'm not sure they believed me all the time."

I kissed Thelma's nose one last time and exited the stall. A hay bale sat across the aisle from her stall, and I sank down on it. "It was the truth most of the time, except..." A smile played on my lips.

"Except?"

"Except the time you hung the tire swing from the hayloft. That was fun. Even the other cowboys joined in on that one."

"I got in so much trouble for that one. It was dangerous."

I shrugged. Still walking down memory lane, I thought about the last summer we had together as teenagers before I left for college. "How about the time we went skinny dipping in the lake?"

Tim had his back to me, so I couldn't see his expression. His ears flamed red, and he dropped his brush. He stammered.

"The police officer was nice. He even offered me a blanket to wrap up in." I went on. "I wonder what would've happened if we didn't get caught." I tilted my head back against the wall and propped up one foot.

He swung around. His gaze hot on me. Emotions swirled in his eyes. My heart stuttered at his expression. He left the stall, closing the door behind him. In two strides, he was beside the bale. His hands pulled me to my feet and drew me into his chest. His pulse jumped in his neck. Heat coursed through me from his touch. My chest constricted with all the emotions I'd ever felt for him.

"I wondered, too." His lips inches from mine. His breath fell on my cheeks. His eyes locked on mine.

I swallowed and licked my lips.

MY FIRST KISMENT CHRISTMAS

His hand moved to the base of my head. He wove his fingers through my hair. "Probably something like this."

His hands brought me close against his chest. Every muscle of his tightened and bunched. His lips closed the gap, falling gently on mine. Fireworks exploded at his touch. Electricity zinged through my body ending in my toes. They curled tightly as he deepened the kiss. I needed him to keep kissing me and holding me. I wrapped my arms around him as I returned the kiss. All the feelings I had ever felt and currently felt for him, I tried to convey. It was a language that only the two of us knew.

Too soon, he pulled back and broke the kiss. I panted for breath and leaned on his arms. The fire in his eyes brighter than before. He rested his forehead against mine. His arms held me as one holds something precious and breakable.

We both knew how it ended all those years. The next day I broke his heart.

Maybe, this was our moving passed everything that happened. Maybe, this was the first step to a new relationship built on maturity, understanding, and real true love. I closed my eyes, enjoying being held, his unique scent enveloping us, the two horses eating hay, and the quiet creaks of the barn. I didn't want to break the moment. I didn't want to let him go. My heart wanted this man more than anything. My mind worried I'd hurt him again or that it was too quick. All I knew was that I was falling in love with Tim Kisment, against all better judgment. Once again.

Aunt Sally sang Christmas carols as Uncle Ernie played the piano after dinner. We were going to the candlelight service at church in a couple of hours. The Christmas lights on the tree gave a soft glow over the darkening living room. The apple pie cooled on the counter, waiting as an after-church treat. It's cinnamon and apple goodness called to me, but I was stuffed from dinner.

I sighed. It was great to be back home with family. Not like my house on the army base. It had been too cold and empty since my husband never came home again. I leaned against the back of the sofa, putting my aching feet up on the ottoman. My mind wandered over the last couple of days with Tim. It was like we were back in high school again, giggling at his jokes and stealing kisses behind the barn. A tingle of excitement went through me. I forgot how much I enjoyed being with him. My hand rubbed circles on my belly where the baby kicked.

The doorbell rang.

"I'll get it." I called to my aunt and uncle.

They waved and continued with their singing. I hefted myself from the deep cushions of the couch and slowly walked to the door. I opened the door.

"Merry Christmas," Tim said. He held out a bouquet of red carnations and baby's breath.

His smile sent a warmth through me all the way to my toes. I sniffed the bouquet.

"These are beautiful. Thank you." I swung the door open wider. "Do you want to come in?"

He glanced past me to where my aunt and uncle were on the piano. He shook his head. "Actually, could you take a walk with me? It is nice out."

"It will be more like a waddle." I reached for my coat.

"No biggie." He helped me into my coat. "I can waddle next to you if that will make you feel better."

I laughed. "No, then people will think something is wrong with you." I swatted his shoulder.

He held out his elbow and I slipped my arm through his. He tucked my arm close to his side, pulling me close. His warmth enveloped me, wrapping me in a safe cocoon.

"Where are we headed?" We stepped off the front porch and onto the sidewalk.

"Let's go see the lights on Main Street," he said as he steered me toward downtown Sunnydale.

I leaned into him, enjoying the quietness of the evening and his company. His boots clopped on the pavement as my tennis shoes squeaked occasionally. The air grew cooler as the sun's rays left. The streetlights flickered on in warm yellow glows. Then all at once, the Christmas lights on Main Street came to light, bathing the street in a fairy tale feeling.

The fronts of the stores and shops were decorated in Christmas themes with Santas, snowmen, and Nativity scenes. Lights wound over the windows and door frames to outline the individual buildings. Wreaths hung on doors with holly and bells. A tall Christmas tree stood in front of the town hall. A group of carolers sang on one side of the tree. A couple of children set up a stand selling hot chocolate with marshmallows. One of the fathers had a flask he was spiking some of the adults' drinks with. Another group of children played tag up and down the street.

Tim squeezed my hand. "Are you happy to be home?"

Home? Sunnydale was my home. I felt like I never left. "Yes, it's great to be back." I took in a deep breath and cringed as a pain wrapped around my body.

"You all right?" He brought me to face him as he scanned me.

I rubbed the side of my belly. "Just breathed too deep I suspect."

He frowned.

"Let's continue on." I slipped my arm back into his and we walked down the street to study the displays.

After a couple of shops, Tim drew me to a wooden bench. We settled onto it holding hands. Our knees bumped together. I rubbed a spot on my belly and shifted my weight. In the window across from us, a train circled around a Christmas tree carrying teddy bears.

Tim cleared his throat. "Um...Judy, I wanted to talk to you."

"About what?" I smiled at the bear on the caboose. He hung off the back in a frozen wave.

"Judy." Tim squeezed both of my hands, bringing my attention to him.

"Everything alright?"

All the laughter and carefree of earlier was gone. Instead, he was serious with an intense look in his eyes.

"Yes, I want to talk to you."

"You said that." I extracted one hand and pressed against the side of my belly. His eyes followed it. "What about?"

"Your situation. I am worried about you."

"My situation?" My temper flared. "Please tell me, what is it your worried about? The baby? Or the fact I'm a widow? Or that I'm at my aunt and uncle's house."

"No, that's not what I meant." He reached for my hand.

I let him take it as I leaned away from him.

"That's not what I meant. It was the wrong word to use."

"Yes, it was." I shot back.

He sighed. His shoulders slumped. "This is harder than I thought. What I meant to say is that I've been thinking about us."

"Us?" I wrinkled my nose at him. "What about us?"

"I was thinking we should get married." He smiled weakly at me.

"What?" I gasped. A few passersby glanced over at us before hurrying on. I yanked at my hands, but he held on.

"Well, it would be good for the baby, and you can live with me. I can take care of you."

"Take care of me? It would be good for the baby? I can't believe you," I seethed. "I can take care of myself. Thank you very much."

"I know you can take care of yourself." He ran his fingers through his hair before covering my hand with his. "It keeps coming out wrong."

"Then say it right." I raised an eyebrow at him. My stomach fluttered and squeezed. I rubbed the heel of my hand down my side. What was he getting at?

He swallowed and looked at our hands. "I know that this is sudden, and we just started seeing each other. But I've always loved you. I want to be your husband and be with you always."

His eyes traveled to mine. I bit my lip. My heart flip-flopped at his words. He loved me? The fluttering in my abdomen increased. I placed my free hand on my stomach. It had been a whirlwind the last few days with him. All of my hormones were up and down, I wasn't sure what was real and what was the pregnancy. Did I enjoy being with him? Of course. Did I want to get remarried? I wasn't sure. It seemed too soon for some reason.

"I don't know," I finally said. "It all seems too quick. How do we know that the feelings are real?"

He deflated like a balloon. "My feelings are real."

"Are they? They aren't just left over from before? I'm really sorry, Tim. I am. I'm just not sure it's for the best." I patted his hands with mine.

He stood up from the bench and pulled me to my feet. "Do me a favor?"

I nodded.

"Think about it tonight and meet me at our spot in the morning at seven o'clock to give me your answer."

"It might not change."

He smiled sadly. "At least, I would know that you thought about it. Come on, let's get you home."

We ambled slowly back the way we came. The Christmas lights seemed to have lost their charm as my mind whirled with his proposal. Think about it about overnight? It seemed dangerous to me. The more I spent time with him, the more I remembered how good we were together before. Was I just in love with what had been? Or did I love the current Tim?

"Here we are," Tim said, interrupting my thoughts. He kissed my knuckles. "Promise me you'll think about it."

"I'll let you know in the morning. My answer may be the same."

"I'll take that risk."

Chapter Nine

Tim

Christmas Day

The hands on my wristwatch moved in slow motion. The minutes inched by with the faint ticking of the watch. I paced back and forth in front of the oak tree with a tree swing. It swung slowly back and forth in the early morning breeze. The ropes creaked and groaned. A cricket played his music in the tall grass. Birds called to one another. The sun began to warm the earth with its rays.

I paced ten steps and turned on my heel and paced another. Back and forth and back and forth. My boots wore a path in the grass. I checked my watch again. Six fifty-eight. A couple more minutes. Thoughts tumbled about in my mind. What if I asked her too soon? What if she didn't believe my feelings for her? What if she thought I was patronizing her?

What if she said no?

I ran a hand through my hair. I couldn't lose her again. Being with her awoke dormant feelings. My love grew and blossomed in her presence. I needed her in my life.

Seven o'clock.

No sign of Judy.

I blew out a sigh, my breath condensing in the cold morning air.

Maybe she was running late.

I returned to my pacing. She'd show up. She would, even if it was just to tell me no. At least, the Judy from high school would.

But.

Did I know her now? She may have changed. My heart still knew her. She was still the independent woman I loved back then.

She would show.

Five minutes.

Ten minutes.

Twenty minutes.

The sun now sat at the horizon and the countryside began to awaken. Bird flew from trees to trees. A rabbit scurried past me. A deer watched me from the stand of trees.

"It's seven-thirty," I muttered as I checked my watch for the hundredth time. "She's not going to show up."

I ran my fingers through my hair. My heart broke. She didn't feel the same way about me as I did about her. It was only my feelings from the past. I pined for her when she left for college. She mustn't have thought about me at all.

My shoulders drooped. I shoved my cowboy hat back on my head. It was time to go to church.

The church bells tolled, calling the late comers to their seats. The little country church was packed. People chatted quietly to each other. They shifted in their seats. A baby cried in the back. Poinsettias covered every available surface, even surrounding the Christmas tree.

Pastor John handed me my Bible. "You've got a full house this morning. You nervous?"

I swallowed the nerves and tugged on my tie. "Just a bit."

"It's Christmas Day. You've prepared for it. You will do great." He patted me on my arm. "Now, I have a few parishioners to see this morning. Thank you for filling in for me."

"No problem." I rubbed the toe of my cowboy boot on my pant leg to remove a smudge. "I'm looking forward to it."

Pastor John left out the back door as the organist began with the first few chords of the opening hymn. That was my cue. I tucked the Bible under my arm and straightened my tie before stepping out in front of my home congregation.

The church service flew by with the ease of a well-oiled machine. Before I knew it, I was shaking hands with the last few members in church.

Mrs. Braun was the last person to leave the church. She was almost a hundred years old and moved very slow, so that she always sat in the back. She walked the few steps to me, pushing her walker. Her daughter and grandson flanked her on either side.

"What a wonderful service today, Tim." She clasped my hand in her frail fingers. She leaned against the side of the walker. "I noticed that some people were missing today."

"I'm sure they were with their families."

"Was there a certain someone that you were expecting?" Her eyes twinkled as she gazed up at me.

My smile fell a bit. Judy didn't come to church, and neither did Ernie nor Sally. "Maybe."

"I don't know if you heard." She motioned me closer. "An ambulance came to the Ernie and Sally White's residence last night."

"An ambulance? Is everything alright?" My heart jumped in my chest.

"Mother, stop scaring the boy." Her daughter stepped in. "We think the baby decided to come. Ernie and Sally haven't been home, yet."

I felt like I had been kicked in the stomach. Judy was having her baby? By herself? The room spun and the voices sounded further away. I placed my hand against the wall behind me, steadying myself. Is that why she didn't show this morning?

"I heard that they went to the San Antonio Hospital," Mrs. Braun said.

"That's what I heard from my friend who's an EMT." Her daughter agreed.

"We better let Tim go." Mrs. Braun winked at me. "He needs to go get some flowers."

"Flowers?" My brain spun, trying to keep up.

"Yes, dear, to give to the new mother." Mrs. Braun smiled. "It's nice to see young people in love"

"Yes, Mother. I think there is someone you need to see." Her daughter assisted her mother a few steps forward.

Judy at the hospital. Judy was having her baby, alone. I needed to be there. I leaned forward and kissed the two women on their cheeks.

"Thank you for telling me," I said. I shook her grandson's hand.

"I'll close up the church, if you want to get going." He leaned away from me as if I was going to kiss him too.

"Thank you," I said. I turned and sprinted to my truck in the parking lot.

The drive to San Antonio went by in slow motion. My truck couldn't go fast enough. Luckily, I didn't meet any police officers on my drive.

The traffic in the city was light. I made it to the hospital without any big delays or traffic jams. I swung my truck into a parking spot. Reaching over to the passenger seat, I slammed my cowboy hat on my head and grabbed the bouquet of flowers I picked up at a gas station. Carnations in pretty colors and some baby's breath.

"Time to go, Tim," I said to myself. "She needs you whether she admits it or not."

The glass doors to the emergency room entrance slid open with a whoosh as I approach. The room was empty of patients and smelled of disinfectant. Quiet music piped over the waiting room. The receptionist sat at her desk reading a romance novel and sipping from a mug. Her eyes pulled up from the page. Her eyebrows raised as she took in the bouquet I was holding.

"Who are you here to see?" She closed the book with a soft thud as she straightened in her seat, all business.

I cleared my throat. Did Judy go by her maiden name or her husband's name? I kicked myself for not asking. "Judy…White…She came in last night." I shifted from foot to foot. "I think she might be in the birthing ward."

"You are?"

"Tim Kisment…her…boyfriend."

Her eyes softened and a pitying look flashed across her face before she turned away. "I'll call up and check. You can take a seat."

"Thank you, ma'am."

She nodded and reached for the telephone.

I made my way over to the hard plastic chairs, my boots echoing on the tile floor in the empty room. The receptionist's voice was barely audible as she talked to someone. The large clock ticked by the seconds. The chair was even more uncomfortable than it looked. I shifted my weight in the chair several times before standing up.

I walked over to the window and looked out across the parking lot. A few people dressed in scrubs entered in a side door. Another car pulled up next to mine and one car left the parking lot. The ambulance barreled out with its lights and siren blaring. The telephone clattered down into its resting spot, drawing my attention to back to the front desk. The receptionist was back to reading her novel.

I sighed. How long would I have to wait? How was Judy doing? Why didn't anyone tell me? What if there was something wrong? What if...

"Tim?" A nurse in pink scrubs appeared at my shoulder.

I nodded.

"Follow me. We were told to expect you." She smiled at me.

I shook my head. Ernie and Sally must have told her.

She led me through a maze of corridors, up in an elevator, and down another hallway to end in a set of double doors. A small Christmas tree sat in the corner covered with glass ornaments and lights. Christmas music played from a radio on the desk where another nurse scribbled in a medical note.

"Here we are. The birthing ward." She pushed through the doors. "She is the fourth door on the right." She nodded to the only closed door.

I swallowed. My stomach twisted in knots with each step. What would I say to her? Would she be happy to see me? I clutched the bouquet in my left hand and raised the right to knock on the door.

My knuckles rapped the door. No answer came from inside. I hesitated. The nurse appeared at my shoulder.

"Go on in. She's probably sleeping." She opened the door and motioned me inside.

The light filtered through the curtains, casting a soft glow in the room. A beam slid through a gap in between the curtains and fell on her face. She slept curled on her side with her hair strewn about her. She was so beautiful she took my breath away. I tiptoed into the room. Another hard plastic chair sat next to the bed. I sunk down in it and laid the flowers across my lap.

Her eyelids fluttered.

"Tim." My name escaped her lips in a sigh. Her hand crept closer to me. "What are you doing here?"

"I needed to see you, Judy." I held her hand with mine.

A faint smile pulled at her lips before her eyes closed once more. Her breathing slowed. She snuggled closer to my side of the bed.

I stroked the back of her hand. There was so much I wanted to tell her. Instead, I watched her sleep. A nurse came in and checked her vitals. She jotted down something in the chart.

"She's going to be fine. She's just exhausted." She smiled at my worried look. "I bet she'll be awake soon."

"How do you know?"

She chuckled. "The baby is going to be hungry."

The baby. I squeezed Judy's hand. She murmured something in her sleep and dozed back again. She did it. She had a baby.

Fifteen minutes later, another nurse came in and gently shook Judy awake.

"Miss, are you ready for the baby?"

She blinked at the smiling nurse before her gaze slid over to me. She removed her hand from mine as she struggled to sit up. Her eyes had dark circles around them, and her hair stuck out at all angles.

"Tim," her voice croaked. "Can you get me some coffee?"

"Absolutely, beautiful." I kissed her forehead and rose from my seat.

She slumped against the pillows.

"Right this way, Mr. Kisment. Our cafeteria is closed for Christmas, but I'll show you where the coffee is." The nurse escorted me out and down the hall.

"Did she have a boy or a girl?" My eyes followed another nurse with a baby bundled in blankets.

"A boy." She smiled at me. "Now let's get your girl some coffee."

Chapter Ten

Judy

Christmas Day

Tim was here, in the hospital. I couldn't believe it. I must have been hallucinating from the drugs they gave me. I closed my eyes. It was just hard to believe. Technically, I stood him up this morning even though I planned on meeting. Plus, this wasn't his baby.

A sighed escaped. We did have a great time together the past few days. A knock sounded on the door and a nurse stuck her head into the room.

"Ready for the baby?"

I scooted myself up on the bed and nodded my head. My little baby boy. My heart squeezed at the sight of his perfect little face. The love for him hurt. Tears welled up in my eyes as I reached for him

"You are perfect. Your daddy would've been so proud," I whispered as I took him from the nurse.

His eyes fluttered opened, and he gave a squawk. I hugged him to my breaking heart.

The nurse laughed. "Let's get him settled."

A few minutes later, the baby slept in my arms. I ran a finger over the fine hair on the top of his head. A knock sounded at the door.

Tim walked into the room in his cowboy boots and jeans, holding two steaming cups. He stopped at the end of my bed. He cleared his throat.

"I brought coffee." He held up the cups with a small grin.

I struggled to shift the sleeping baby so I could sit up more. Tim placed the cups on the table next to my bed.

"Do you mind if I take him?" He extended his big hands.

I hugged the baby closer and searched Tim's face. Did he really want to hold the baby? Could I give the baby up? Tim's eyes spoke to my soul, assuring me that everything was going to be fine. I placed the baby in Tim's hands. He cradled the baby close to him before sitting in the spare chair.

The baby opened his eyes and blinked up at Tim. Tim smiled down at him. It was such a tender moment. I couldn't hold back the tears. They flowed from my eyes and ran in rivers down my cheeks.

"Are you okay?" Tim leaned closer to me. "I can give him back."

"No. It's not that." I dashed at the tears. "The moment is perfect."

Tim's face split into a large grin as he gazed down at the baby. "He's perfect. You did a great job." He leaned over the baby and placed a kiss to the baby's forehead. "I love him already."

More tears streamed from my cheeks. My heart was so full of love it felt ready to burst. I wiped at them. Tim stood up and placed the baby back into my arms. I cuddled the baby close to me as I sunk back onto the hospital bed. Tim gazed down at us. A smile tugged at the corners of his lips. He swept the cowboy hat from his head and gripped the brim.

"What did you name him?" He whispered.

"Kaleb, after his father." I kissed the top of his head. "I wish he knew that he was going to be a father." I raised my eyes to Tim. "My little boy won't have one."

Tim's eyes held mine. His soul called to mine. I wanted him, but how could I ask him to be my husband and a father after everything I put him through. Being with him the last couple of days, my love for him emerged from where I buried it all those years ago. Did he love me enough to be a part our lives? It was a lot to ask of anyone. Part of me wished that this was his baby, and he would be with me forever.

Tim swallowed and placed his cowboy hat on the chair next to him. He grabbed my free hand and knelt on one knee.

"Tim?" I tried to pull him up. What was he doing? Was this for real? "What are you doing?"

"Judy, let me say my piece." He tucked a stray hair behind my ear. My skin tingled under his touch. "I can't replace the man you lost. I won't even try." He cleared his throat. "I have loved you since high school. Even when you left, I tried to move on, but my heart compared every woman to you. These past couple of days were a dream come true and I'm afraid to wake up and find you gone again. I promise you that I will love you with all of my heart and love baby Kaleb as if he was my own."

I couldn't believe it. I couldn't breathe. My chest ached as I hung on every one of his words.

"Will you make me the happiest man by marrying me?"

More tears fell from my eyes. "Are you sure?"

"Yes, I want you both in my life." Hope filled his eyes.

I nodded my head. "I can't wait to be your wife."

Tim gave a quiet whoop as he stood up. His hand cupped my cheek bringing my lips to his. They touched with a spark of passion. The spark lit a fire that consumed me. The kiss deepened, drawing me out of myself, losing myself to the passion.

Kaleb wiggled in my arms and gave a small squawk. Tim broke the kiss. His lips pressed against my temple as he pulled away.

"Quiet, little one," I hushed the baby.

Tim dug in his pocket and pulled out a velvet covered box.

"I hoped you'd say yes." He opened the box.

The small diamond sparkled in the hospital lights as it sat on top of the soft gold band.

I gasped. "It is beautiful."

He smiled and took it out of the box. He slid it on my finger where it fit just right. I extended my hand out to the light, admiring the diamond.

"Just like you." His lips touched my temple, lightly pressing against my skin.

I sighed and scooted over in the bed to give him room. He perched on the side of the bed and wrapped his arm around Kaleb and me.

"Our little family," he whispered in my ear.

I snuggled against his strong chest as his muscular arms held me. Everything was right in the world. "When do you want to get married?"

He chuckled into my hair. "As soon as possible. I've waited forever for this moment."

I sighed and closed my eyes. Contentment flowed through me. My baby slept in my arms while my man held me in his. His chest rose and fell in time with mine. Our two hearts seemed to beat as one. It had been a long time since I felt love like this.

A knock sounded at the door and a nurse entered.

"Sorry to interrupt." She smiled at us. "But it's snowing outside." She hurried across to the windows and drew the curtains.

Tim slid from the bed and helped me up. Kaleb snuggled against my shoulder as I made my way over to the window. Tim stood behind me, his arms wrapped around both of us. Big fluffy flakes floated down from the gray skies. They landed lightly on the picnic table outside of my window. Someone turned on the Christmas lights in the picnic area. They twinkled through the snowflakes.

"It is magical," I said.

Tim tightened his arms around us. "Merry Christmas, my love."

"Merry Christmas, Tim. Our first Christmas together."

Epilogue

Judy

Present Day

"That was our first Christmas of many," Tim said after I finished my part. He squeezed my shoulder. "Every Christmas after has been wonderful."

We shared a smile and I leaned into him. Our lips touched for a moment, sharing our love for each other after all these years. I couldn't believe how lucky I was to have a second chance with this man.

"I didn't know that you have a different dad," Erin said to Kaleb.

Kaleb shrugged. "It doesn't matter. Pa has been the best dad I could've asked for." He turned his attention to me. "I did visit his grave once."

"You did?" I asked, surprised.

"I was on that trip to Virginia for college. I stopped by the cemetery and found his grave site. I left some change and flowers on his headstone," Kaleb said.

"That was very nice," I choked out the words. I wiped a tear from my eyes. Tim rubbed my back gently. Even after all these years, some hurts never heal. Losing a husband was one of those.

"Hey everyone," Katie stood back from the window and let the drape fall back into place. "Come outside!" She grabbed Levi's hand and dragged him to the front door. He laughed at her but went with her. He grabbed her camera from a side table.

We crowded on to the porch. Katie spun in a slow circle with her arms outstretch. Large snowflakes fell on to her hands and in her hair. Levi snapped photos of her.

A blanket of white covered the ground. Kade whooped and jumped over the railing of the porch. The snow exploded around him when he landed. He packed a handful of snow into ball.

"Snowball fight!" He launched the first snowball.

It landed with a splat against Kurt's shirt, melting on impact. "Hey!" He climbed over the railing and landed in the snow a few feet away from Kade. He scooped up a fist full of snow.

Kaleb, Levi, Katie, and Erin joined them in a flurry of wet snowballs. Laughter filled the air as they ran around chasing each other like kids.

"Merry Christmas, my love," Tim whispered in my ear.

"That it is." I turned in his arms. "Everything is perfect."

Our lips met with an explosion of fireworks. I sunk into his embrace as our hearts shared our love for each other and the wonderful family that we made together.

To read about Judy and Tim's wedding, join my newsletter at alliebock.substack.com[1].

---

1. http://alliebock.substack.com/

If you enjoyed this story, please leave a review! This helps other readers find the story. Thank you!

Don't miss out!

Visit the website below and you can sign up to receive emails whenever Allie Bock publishes a new book. There's no charge and no obligation.

https://books2read.com/r/B-A-HTMK-PPBEC

BOOKS 2 READ

Connecting independent readers to independent writers.

Did you love *My First Kisment Christmas*? Then you should read *My Cowboy of Convenience*[2] by Allie Bock!

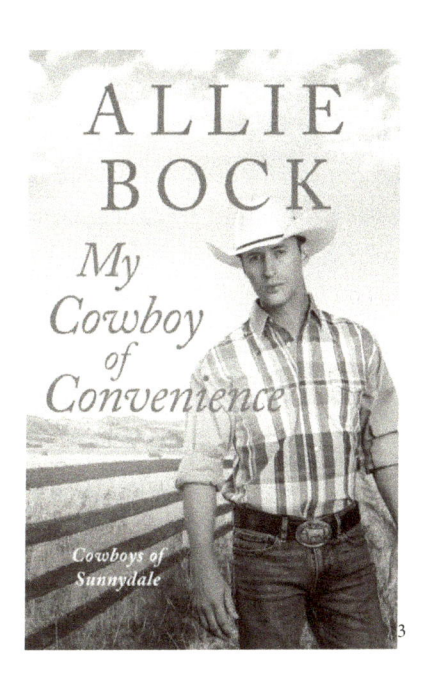

No Dating Clients

I needed a change: a new job, new friends, a new life. Something different, especially after my fiancé left me at the altar to go on my honeymoon with my best friend.

That's how I found myself across the country in a small town in Texas as the new veterinarian. The only rule my new boss was firm on was 'no dating clients'. Not a problem for me. I did not need another heartache.

---

2. https://books2read.com/u/m26rjr

3. https://books2read.com/u/m26rjr

But then, I met the handsome ranch owner of the Kisment Ranch. The biggest client we have. He needed a date for his little sister's wedding. A paid date. So, I agreed.

How hard could it be? Go to the wedding and dance with a good-looking cowboy. All without falling in love with him. My heart won't betray me, right?

My Cowboy of Convenience is a standalone in the Cowboys of Sunnydale Series with a slow-burn romance with adventure. Saddle up for a page-turning ride!

Read more at https://www.alliebock.com.

Also by Allie Bock

Cowboys of Sunnydale
My Cowboy Crush
Falling For My Cowboy
Second Chance with My Bull Rider
My Unexpected Hero
My Cowboy of Convenience
My First Kisment Christmas

Watch for more at https://www.alliebock.com.

About the Author

After living all over the country, Allie resides in Minnesota where she spends the daylight hours working as an equine veterinarian. In the evening, she escapes to imaginary Sunnydale, Texas. She loves to write about strong heroines who overcome challenges to fall in love with handsome cowboys.

Follow her on Substack at alliebock.substack.com or visit her website at alliebock.com.

When she is not working or writing, she can be found reading and spending time with the love of her life, their little kids, and their Dachshund. When they aren't in the house, they are riding their horses across open fields.

Read more at https://www.alliebock.com.

Milton Keynes UK
Ingram Content Group UK Ltd.
UKHW041948291124
451915UK00001B/48